A Note to Parents

Read to your child...

★ Reading aloud is one of the best ways to develop your child's love of reading. Read together at least 20 minutes each day.

★ Laughter is contagious! Read with feeling. Show your child that reading is fun.

★ Take time to answer questions your child may have about the story. Linger over pages that interest your child.

...and your child will read to you.

★ Follow cues from your child to know when he wants to join in the reading.

★ Support your young reader. Give him a word whenever he asks for it.

★ Praise your child as he progresses. Your encouraging words will build his confidence.

You can help your Level 1 reader.

★ Reading begins with knowing how a book works. Show your child the title and where the story begins.

★ Ask your child to find picture clues on each page. Talk about what is happening in the story.

★ Point to the words as you read so your child can make the connection between the print and the story.

★ Ask your child to point to words she knows.

★ Let your child supply the rhyming words.

Most of all, enjoy your reading time together!

—Bernice Cullinan, Ph.D.,
Professor of Reading, New York University

Fisher-Price and related trademarks and copyrights are used under
license from Fisher-Price, Inc., a subsidiary of Mattel, Inc.,
East Aurora, NY 14052 U.S.A.
©2003, 2000 Mattel, Inc.
All Rights Reserved. **MADE IN CHINA**.
Published by Reader's Digest Children's Books
Reader's Digest Road, Pleasantville, NY U.S.A. 10570-7000
Copyright © 2000 Reader's Digest Children's Publishing, Inc.
All rights reserved. Reader's Digest Children's Books is a trademark
and Reader's Digest and All-Star Readers are registered trademarks of
The Reader's Digest Association, Inc.
Conforms to ASTM F963 and EN 71
10

Library of Congress Cataloging-in-Publication Data

Shook, Babs.
    A house for mouse / by Babs Shook ; illustrated by Kathy Couri.
        p. cm. — (All-star readers. Level 1)
    Summary: Several animals offer to let a little mouse live with
them, but he keeps searching until he finds just the right home.
    ISBN 1-57584-383-8 (alk. paper)
    [1. Mice Fiction. 2. Animals—Habitations Fiction. 3. Stories in rhyme.]
I. Couri, Kathryn A., ill. II. Title. III. Series.
PZ8.3.S55915Ho   2000   [E] — dc21   99-34957

A House for Mouse

by Babs Shook
illustrated by Kathy Couri

1
All-Star Readers®
Reader's Digest Children's Books™
Pleasantville, New York • Montréal, Québec

I am a mouse,
a little mouse.

I need a house,
a little house.

I need a house,
a place to be.

I need a friend
to be with me.

A fish says, "Come. Come live with me.

Come share my house.
It's in the sea."

I shake my head.

I say to him,
"I cannot come.
I cannot swim."

A bird says, "Come.
Come live with me.

Come share my house.
It's in a tree."

15

"Oh, dear!" I say,
"I cannot fly.
Your house is nice,
but it's too high."

And then I see a little house.

It looks just right
for a little mouse.

And then I hear
somebody shout,
"Can you please come
and help me out?"

I go inside.
What do I see?

A little mouse—
a mouse like me.

He says, "I need
to paint my house.

But it's too hard
for just one mouse!"

"It's not too hard for two," I say.

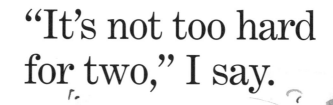

"I like to paint.
May I please stay?"

Today I am
a happy mouse.

I have a nice new friend and house.

Color in the star next to each word you can read.

☆ a	☆ have	☆ may	☆ see
☆ am	☆ he	☆ me	☆ shake
☆ and	☆ head	☆ mouse	☆ share
☆ be	☆ hear	☆ my	☆ shout
☆ bird	☆ help	☆ need	☆ somebody
☆ but	☆ high	☆ new	☆ stay
☆ can	☆ him	☆ nice	☆ swim
☆ cannot	☆ house	☆ not	☆ the
☆ come	☆ I	☆ oh	☆ then
☆ dear	☆ in	☆ one	☆ to
☆ do	☆ inside	☆ out	☆ today
☆ fish	☆ is	☆ paint	☆ too
☆ fly	☆ it	☆ place	☆ tree
☆ for	☆ just	☆ please	☆ two
☆ friend	☆ like	☆ right	☆ what
☆ go	☆ little	☆ say	☆ with
☆ happy	☆ live	☆ says	☆ you
☆ hard	☆ looks	☆ sea	☆ your